THE GHOST ON SATURDAY NIGHT

Black seconds ticked away. Then a minute or two. Professor Pepper became as short-tempered as a teased snake.

"Rise up, I say!" he commanded. "I've a hanging rope in my hand! Aye, and I'll string you up a *fourth* time!"

Silence.

And then there came a creaking of wood. And a groaning of nails. My neck went cold and prickly. *The lid of that pine coffin was lifting!*

THE GHOST ON SATURDAY NIGHT

by Sid Fleischman

Illustrated by Laura Cornell

A Beech Tree Paperback Book New York

The text type is ITC Century Light.

Library of Congress Cataloging in Publication Data
Fleischman, Sid, (date)
The ghost on Saturday night / by Sid Fleischman ; pictures by Laura Cornell.
p. cm.
Summary: When Professor Pepper gives Ople tickets to a ghost-raising
instead of a nickel in payment for being guided through the dense
fog, Ople manages to make money anyway by helping
to thwart a bank robbery.
ISBN 0-688-14919-7 (trade). — ISBN 0-688-14920-0 (pbk.)
[1. Ghost—Fiction. 2. West (U.S.)—Fiction.
3. Robbers and outlaws—Fiction.] I. Cornell, Laura, ill. II. Title.
PZ7.F5992Gk 1997 [Fic]—dc20 96-43551 CIP AC

First Beech Tree Edition, 1997
Published by arrangement with the author

13 14 15 LP/OPM 10 9 8

In memory of
Bill Grote

CONTENTS

CONTENTS

1

FOG

There's nothing bashful about a tule fog. It'll creep inside your clothes. It'll seep through the window cracks and get right into bed with you.

When I got home from the schoolhouse on Tuesday, there wasn't a wisp of fog. I lived with my great-aunt Etta and she was waiting for me.

"Opie," she said. "How would you like chicken for supper?"

"Yes, *ma'am!*" I said.

"Splendid. I've got the chicken. You go out back and pluck it."

I gave a groan. She gave me the chicken. She had a way of foxing me into doing pesky chores like that.

I sat myself on the chopping stump and began to pull feathers. I passed the time thinking up names for my horse. I already had a list a mile-and-a-half long.

I didn't own a horse—yet.

But I had one promised. Aunt Etta had struck a bargain with me. When I earned enough money to buy a good saddle, she'd buy a good horse to fit under it.

The trouble was I was only ten and kind of runty in size. The older, bigger boys seemed to get all the after-school jobs around town.

"Wild Charlie," I said aloud. I liked the sound of that. A horse ought to have the exact right name. I mean, you wouldn't name a fine horse Hubert. He'd die of shame.

I could see myself galloping across the meadow on Wild Charlie. But when I looked up I couldn't see the meadow. Or the trees. Or the barn. And before long I couldn't even see the chicken in my hands.

A tule fog had sprung up.

My heart gave a mighty leap. There was saddle money to be made in a good thick fog! I had already saved $2.11. But I needed

heaps and heaps of money—$17.59 exactly.

I began plucking the rest of those feathers so fast you'd think that hen was in a rooster fight. The fog around me was dripping wet. All you needed to wash your ears was a bar of soap. Not that I had a mind to.

I guess there's nothing thicker and wetter than a ground-hugging California tule fog. Aunt Etta was always saying not to stand in one too long. You'd grow webbed feet.

I felt my way back to the house and handed the bird to Aunt Etta.

"I'll be back for supper," I said.

"Don't you got lost," she said. "That tule is so thick you'll need a compass to cross the road."

"Yes, ma'am."

"And don't stay out too long. You'll grow webbed feet."

2
THE GHOST IS COMING!

I lifted my feet for town. I guess I was the only boy in Golden Hill who'd gone into the fog business. I'd gotten the idea from Aunt Etta herself.

Even in the thickest tule she was sure-footed as a mountain goat. She knew every brick, every post, and every building by heart. So did I. I could streak through town with my eyes shut.

I passed one end of the old Horseshoe Mine tunnel. I couldn't see it, but I knew it

was there because of the dip in the road. Before long I reached the hotel hitching rack. I crossed the dirt street and counted forty-seven strides. That brought me to Muldoon's General Store.

"Any special errands you want run, Mr. Muldoon?" I asked. He was one of my best tule customers.

"Opie," he said, "if that fog gets any thicker you could drive a nail in it and hang your coat. Think you can find the barbershop?"

"Yes, sir."

He filled a can with lamp oil and I set out to deliver it. I turned the corner and kept going until I reached the livery stable—I knew it by the smell. Then I crossed the street. When I sniffed hair tonic I knew I was at Ed Russell's barbershop.

It turned out there was a stranger in

town. Mr. Russell had just finished cutting his hair.

"Opie," he said, "you could do this gentleman a service if you scouted him back to the hotel."

"Be pleased to," I said.

That stranger was a big man and uglier than homemade soap. He clasped my shoulder

with one hand as I led him out along the wooden sidewalk. That hand of his was cold. It felt like ice melting on my shoulder.

He followed along behind me without saying a word.

I didn't say much either. He was kind of scary. But when we passed the bank I said, "You ever hear of anyone buying a horse with a penny?"

He didn't answer.

"Well, sir, that's what my great-aunt Etta is going to do," I added.

He wasn't interested—that was clear. So I didn't tell him it wasn't a common, ordinary Indian-head cent you might find in your pocket. It was an 1877 Indian-head penny. Rare as a hen's tooth, that date. And mighty valuable. She had Mr. Whitman, the banker, keep it in his safe. She was always worried that she'd spend it by mistake.

"Here we are, sir," I said. We reached the hotel porch. He lifted that freezing claw of his off my shoulder. I was glad to be rid of him. But I hoped I would be a nickel closer to my saddle.

He dug in his vest pocket. He handed me a card. And he disappeared through the door.

I was sorely disappointed. He was not only big and ugly; he was stingy, too. What did I want his card for?

It was kind of hard to read in the fog. The sun was giving off about as much light as an orange cat. But as I held it closer I saw that it wasn't a calling card. It was a ticket of some sort.

Admit Two
Compliments of Professor Pepper

Admit two to what? Not a word about that. I might have thrown it away if I weren't so puzzled. I jammed it into my back pocket and went about my fog business.

By the time I reached home I had the jingle of thirty-five cents in my pocket. I hoped the tule fog would hang on for weeks.

But it lifted around noon the next day.
And all over town signs had been tacked up.

THE GHOST IS COMING!

See the ghost of Crookneck John!

Famous Outlaw
Murderer
Bank Robber
Thief & Scoundrel

✠ ✠ ✠ Hung three times before he croaked!

THE GENUINE GHOST

Brought back by Professor Pepper, the famous ghost-raiser. Don't miss this event. Startling! Educational! Ladies welcome. No children under twelve allowed.

Saturday Night	**Miners' Union Hall**
8 p.m. sharp	**50 cents Admission**

3

SATURDAY NIGHT

Professor Pepper! I could still feel the chilly clasp of his hand on my shoulder.

I ran home and showed my ticket to Aunt Etta.

"He gave it to me himself!" I said.

"Who did?"

"Professor Pepper. He's a famous ghost-raiser!"

She looked at me over the tops of her glasses. "What on earth is a ghost-raiser?"

"Haven't you seen the signs? He's going to raise the ghost of Crookneck John on Saturday night. Right here in Miners' Union Hall."

"Poppycock," Aunt Etta said.

"The signs say so. The genuine ghost, too."

"I'll believe that when I see it," she snorted.

"Ladies are welcome," I said. And then I added with disappointment, "But they won't let me in."

"Why not?"

"I'm not old enough."

Aunt Etta stared at me. I didn't have to tell her how much I wanted to have a peek at the ghost of Crookneck John. She could see that for herself.

"Well, I'm old enough for both of us," she said. "We'll go."

"But Aunt Etta—"

"You don't think I'd visit a spook show *alone,* Opie. Why, I might faint. We'll see it together. That's that. Leave it to me."

I thought Saturday would never come.

Everyone at school was talking about the ghost of Crookneck John. Talking about sneaking in, mostly. The trouble was there was no way to sneak into the Miners' Union Hall. It stood over the bank. The only way to get up there was by climbing a stairway along the side of the building.

I didn't want to tell anyone that I might be seeing Professor Pepper do his ghost-raising. Aunt Etta wouldn't try to pass me off for twelve years of age—that would be dishonest. I could see myself climbing those stairs with her and being turned away at the door.

Thursday and Friday passed and I didn't think up one new name for my horse. I didn't even look at the Sears, Roebuck catalog. It had a picture of the $17.59 Winfield Special stock saddle. That's the one I was saving up for.

Saturday morning arrived at last.

Then it was Saturday afternoon.

Then it was Saturday night.

Aunt Etta put on her hat and we set out for the Miners' Union Hall.

4

TICKETS FOR TWO

We climbed the wooden stairs to the hall. A toad-faced man stood at the door. He was taking folks' money and tossing it into a cigar box.

When he saw me he shook his head. "That boy ain't old enough to be twelve," he said.

"Correct," Aunt Etta said.

"Then he can't go in."

"Nonsense," she said.

"Ma'am, that ghost will scare him skinny."

"He's already skinny."

"Then his hair will turn white," the man said.

"Horsefeathers, sir." She handed him my ticket from Professor Pepper himself. "Will you kindly read that."

"It says admit two."

Aunt Etta straightened to her full height. "Exactly. I'm *one* and he's *two*. And the ticket orders you to *admit* us. Step aside, sir, before I call the sheriff."

That man turned white as an oyster at the mention of the sheriff.

"Come along, Opie," Aunt Etta said.

We breezed right through the door. Oh, she was clever as forty crickets, my great-aunt Etta.

The hall was long and shadowy. Two oil lamps burned and smoked in front of the curtain. That's all the light there was.

We took chairs near the front and waited. Before long all the chairs were taken. And folks were standing along the walls.

"It's past eight o'clock," Aunt Etta announced.

We could hear noises behind the curtain. There were creaking sounds. And sawing sounds. And hammering sounds

"Maybe it's the ghost," I said.

Aunt Etta shook her head. "Crookneck John was an outlaw—not a carpenter."

We waited. And waited some more.

At ten minutes to nine Professor Pepper stepped through the curtains.

5

PROFESSOR PEPPER

"I will ask the ladies not to scream out," he announced in a deep voice.

"Moonshine," Aunt Etta whispered.

Professor Pepper took a grip on the lapel of his black frock coat. "What you will see tonight is stranger than strange. Odder than odd. Aye, a man deader than dead will walk among you. A cutthroat, he was. Bank robber. The most feared outlaw of the century!"

I began to scrunch down in my chair. I couldn't help it.

"Hung once, he was," Professor Pepper went on. "Hung twice, he was. Hung three times before the meanness was jerked out of him! Aye, that's how he came to be known as Crookneck John."

"I don't wonder," Aunt Etta muttered. "Opie, sit up straight."

Professor Pepper lowered his heavy brows. "I would advise the fainthearted to leave before the ghost-raising begins."

He paused. Everyone seemed to look at everyone else. I saw the Widow Sellers rise and hurry for the door, fanning her face with a handkerchief.

"Now, then, I must have absolute silence!" Professor Pepper said. He clapped his hands sharply.

The curtains parted.

A pine coffin was stretched across two sawhorses. It looked old and rotted, as if it had been dug out of the ground.

"Aye, the very box holding the bones of Crookneck John," the professor declared. "The coffin is six feet long. Crookneck John was almost seven feet. Buried with his knees bent up, he was. Most uncomfortable even for a ghost."

Then Professor Pepper clapped his hands again. His assistant, the toad-faced man, appeared and blew out the two oil lamps.

Pitch darkness closed in on the hall.

For a moment, I don't think anyone took a breath.

Professor Pepper's voice came rolling through the blackness.

"Crookneck John," he called. "I have your bones. Is the spirit willing to come forth, eh? Give a sign."

Silence. All I could hear was my own heart beating. Then there came a hollow rap-rap-rapping from the pine box.

"Aye, I hear the knock of your big knuckles, Mr. Crookneck John. Now rise up. Rise up your bloody bones and stretch your legs, sir."

My eyes strained to see through the darkness.

A minute went by. Maybe two or three. When Professor Pepper spoke again he was getting impatient.

"Rise up, you scoundrel! Ashamed to show your crooked neck to these honest folks, eh? This is Professor Pepper himself speaking. Aye, and I won't be made a fool of, sir!"

Black seconds ticked away. Then a minute or two. Professor Pepper became as short-tempered as a teased snake.

"Rise up, I say!" he commanded. "I've a hanging rope in my hand! Aye, and I'll string you up a *fourth* time!"

Silence.

And then there came a creaking of wood. And a groaning of nails. My neck went cold and prickly. *The lid of that pine coffin was lifting!*

"That's better, you murdering scum!" snarled Professor Pepper.

It was scary to hear him talk that way to a dangerous outlaw about to rise from his coffin.

"I can't make out a thing," Aunt Etta said.

I stared hard, wanting to see that seven-foot ghost stretch his legs.

But suddenly the snarl went out of Professor Pepper's voice. "No! No!" he gasped. "Down! Back, sir! Not the rope!" Gurgling sounds escaped from his throat. "Help! Help! The lamps! Light the la—!"

I was sitting so straight by then I must have shot up six inches taller. The toad-faced man struck a match to the nearest lamp.

The air lit up. And there, against the curtain, staggered Professor Pepper. A hangman's noose was pulled tight around his neck.

The lid of the coffin stood open.

Professor Pepper clawed at the rope around his throat and caught a breath. "Save yourselves!" he croaked. "Run for your lives! Lock your doors! Shut your windows! Stay off the streets! The Crookneck Ghost is loose!"

6

THE COFFIN OF CROOKNECK JOHN

I don't know how many ladies screamed. But three fainted and had to be carried out.

"Come on, Aunt Etta!" I said.

She was calm as an owl at midnight. "Sit where you are."

The hall emptied in a whirlwind hurry. Even the toad-faced man was gone.

There was no one left but Professor Pepper and us.

"Madam," he said. He'd freed himself of the hangman's rope and was hammering the lid back on the coffin. "Your lives are in terrible danger!"

"Pish-posh," she answered. "I'll expect you to refund everyone's money, sir."

At that, he banged his thumb with the hammer. "What!"

"Other folks paid at the door to *see* a ghost. They have been flimflammed."

"Really, madam!"

"*I* didn't see a ghost. *Opie* didn't see a ghost. No one *saw* that ghost of yours."

He stopped shaking the pain out of his thumb. "Unfortunately, madam, my assistant appears to have flown for his life. And with the cigar box full of money. Why, it wouldn't surprise me if we find him with his neck broke and robbed by that thieving ghost."

"Pay up, sir," was all Aunt Etta would say. "Come along, Opie."

"Hold on," Professor Pepper said with sudden politeness. "I've been near strangled. Aye, short of breath I am. Perhaps that fine lad will help me carry the pine box downstairs."

I wasn't anxious to get *that* close to either Professor Pepper or the coffin.

"What on earth for?" Aunt Etta said.

"Why, Crookneck John must return to his

dry bones before the crow of dawn, madam. That's the way of ghosts, you know. I'll have the burying box moved to the jailhouse. He'll wake up behind bars, the scoundrel! Aye, with the cigar box, if he has it."

Then he turned an eye on me. "I'll reward you for your trouble, lad. Cash money."

It wouldn't be much if I knew him, but cash money was saddle money.

"Yes, sir," I answered.

Aunt Etta could read my thoughts. "I've seen enough playacting for one night," she said. "It's past my bedtime. I'm going home, Opie."

"I won't be long," I said.

That pine box was heavy. I didn't think dry old bones could weigh so much. Then I reminded myself that Crookneck John had been seven feet tall.

The moon was rising and full.

When we struggled down to the foot of the stairs Professor Pepper's breath gave out.

"This'll do, lad," he said. "Oh, I should have known better than to raise the Crookneck Ghost on a full moon night. Turns him wild."

Then he dug in his coat pocket and handed me a coin. A mighty small one.

"Run home fast as you can, hear? Make sure that fine lady of yours is safe. I'll manage for myself."

"Much obliged for the cash money," I said politely. But I could tell from the feel it was only a cent piece.

I didn't run home. I wasn't worried about Aunt Etta. She'd said it was all playacting. Professor Pepper *himself* could have done the rap-rap-rapping on the coffin. And he could have tied the noose around his *own* neck.

I wasn't even past the hotel when the moon faded out of the sky. The tule fog was creeping back.

I gave the cent piece a flip in the air and caught it. I put it in my pocket and then took it out again. Awfully clean and shiny, I thought, as if it had never been in use. Like

Aunt Etta's rare Indian-head penny in the bank safe.

There was just enough moonlight left to make out the date.

My breath caught. It was an 1877 Indian-head cent.

7
THE PENNY

The tule fog came seeping up around me. It appeared to be Aunt Etta's very own penny, I thought. The penny that was going to buy a horse to fit under my saddle!

But how had it come to be in Professor Pepper's coat pocket?

Just then I heard the snort of a horse and the creaking of wagon wheels.

"Bah! This fog's so thick I couldn't find my nose with both hands and a lantern."

I knew that voice. It belonged to Professor Pepper's assistant.

"I'm not interested in your nose, idiot!" It was the snarl of Professor Pepper himself. "Find the road. And quick before this town has the law on us."

The law? Suddenly I knew the only way Aunt Etta's rare cent could have gotten into the professor's pocket.

He'd robbed the bank!

"Give me those fool reins," he growled.

I had to do something. I felt my way along the hotel hitching post until I could make out the faint glow of their wagon lamp.

"Stop, sir!" I called out. "You're heading straight into a tree. Need help?"

"Help indeed!" said Professor Pepper. "Where's the road out of town, eh?"

Then he paused.

"Don't I know that voice?"

I was having a time to keep my teeth from clacking now. "Yes, sir," I said. "I'm Opie. I scouted you from the barbershop to the hotel in a thicker fog than this."

"Well, take that nag by the nose and lead us out of here. When Crookneck John wakes up in the jailhouse he'll be after my blood."

More playacting, I thought! Oh, he was full of tricks. He'd scared folks into staying off the streets while he got away. But he hadn't counted on the tule fog.

Or me. An idea had already sprung into my head.

I led the horse and wagon step by step along the road toward home. When I came to the dip, I stopped. We were at one end of the old Horseshoe Mine.

"There's a big tunnel on the left, sir. About

two miles long. It's kind of a shortcut through the fog."

"Aye, a shortcut would please me!" the professor laughed.

A moment later they went clattering into the mine tunnel.

I was in such a hurry to reach Mr. Whitman's house that I must have barked my shins six times and run into a wall at least once.

Mr. Whitman owned the bank. I showed him Aunt Etta's 1877 one-cent piece. I told him I thought Professor Pepper had robbed the safe. And we went for the sheriff.

Sure enough, the bank safe was empty.

"But the walls of the bank are solid stone," Mr. Whitman said. "How did he get in?"

I had already noticed bits of sawdust. I looked up. The sheriff looked up.

"Yup," he said. "Professor Pepper cut through the floor of the Miners' Union Hall upstairs. Probably let himself down with the hangman's rope and up again. Then hammered the wood back in place."

I remembered hearing hammer sounds behind the curtain during the long wait for the show to start.

"And he must have hoped we'd believe it was the Crookneck Ghost who'd robbed the bank," the sheriff said. "Well, Professor Pepper can't have got far in this fog."

"Not far at all," I said. "He's in the Horseshoe Mine."

"The Horseshoe Mine!" the sheriff said.

"Yes, sir."

"Doesn't he know it makes a perfect horseshoe and comes out about forty feet from the jailhouse?"

"No, sir," I said. "I didn't tell him that."

8
CAPTURED!

The end of the tunnel was dark as a sack of black cats. The sheriff waited. His three deputies waited. And I waited, too.

Before long we could hear the echo of horse's hooves. My heart began to beat a little faster. The glow of a lantern appeared like a firefly deep in the tunnel.

The sheriff lifted his shotgun and nodded to his deputies. "Get ready, boys. The rest of you stay back."

The wagon lantern grew larger and brighter. Then I could see Professor Pepper himself—chuckling and singing.

But when he saw the law waiting for him he gave a gasp and a groan.

"Great jumping hop-toads!" he cried out. He grabbed the reins and tried to turn the wagon around. But the mine shaft wasn't wide enough. He kept snapping the whip, but all the horse could do was snort and whinny.

The sheriff charged forward and caught the horse by the halter.

"That will do, gents," he said. "Welcome back to Golden Hill. Easy, now, or you'll end up buckshot ghosts."

"Thunder and lightning," the professor snarled. "We've been out-foxed!"

His helper was still clutching the cigar box full of flimflam money. The deputies led him away, together with Professor Pepper.

The sheriff climbed on the wagon and called to me.

"Opie. Did you say this coffin was uncommon heavy?"

"Yes, sir."

"Hold the lantern."

As I held the lantern he pried off the lid. There were no bones in that pine box at all.

It was full of money. The stolen bank money.

9
THE REWARD

The sheriff looked through his reward posters.

"Sorry, Opie," he said finally. "There's no reward offered for Professor Pepper. You do deserve one."

"That's all right," I said. "I got Aunt Etta's penny back for her. Rare as a hen's tooth, that penny. She's going to buy me a horse with it someday."

Mr. Whitman was sitting nearby counting

the stolen money. He looked up. "A horse," he said. "Well, a horse has got to have something on it."

When I got home from school on Monday a saddle was waiting for me in the parlor. The whole room smelled of fresh leather.

"Aunt Etta," I said. "That's the finest looking saddle I *ever* saw!"

"Not much use without a horse under it," she said. "I've already plucked a chicken for supper. If you've got nothing better to do we could go looking for your horse."

"Yes, ma'am!"

"You might start thinking up a name."

"Aunt Etta," I said, "I've got a list a mile-and-a-half long."